Cynthia Hickey

Poinsettia Madness

A Shady Acres Mystery, Book 4

By Cynthia Hickey

ISBN-13:978-1-0881-5711-4

To My fans and family. My your Christmas be blessed and full of surprises. Not the deadly kind ☺

1

"Shelby Hart, as beautiful as ever."

I straightened from planting the last poinsettia in a sea of red to face my ex. "Well, if isn't Donald Trayer." I lifted my chin. I wouldn't smile or shake his hand. Not after he'd ditched me at the altar months ago. Several Shady Acres residents watched, curiosity etched on their faces. It wasn't often a man other than my new love, Heath McLeroy, spoke with me. Unless it was a police officer, that is.

"How are you?" He tilted his head.

"Peachy. You?" What was he doing here?

"Well, I'm getting married." He grinned.

"To the woman you left me for?" What, he wanted a congratulations?

"No, that didn't work out. My bride-to-be is Sasha Woodrow."

I raised my eyebrows. Donald did get around. My best friend Cheryl Leroix kept me abreast of things that went on at the elementary school where I used to work. "What do you want? I'm busy."

"Well," he took a deep breath. "I, uh, can I have back the jewelry I gave you?"

At least he had the decency to look ashamed.

"I sold it at a yard sale."

"What?" He jerked, his face as red as the Christmas plants behind me. "Do you know how much they were worth?" He ran his hands through his hair. "I can't believe even you could be that stupid!"

"They weren't worth anything to me, and you had given them to me as gifts. That meant I could do with them as I pleased." I eyed the three pronged garden tool in my wheelbarrow. If he got aggressive...

"I ought to ring your..." he growled and turned away. "Of all the idiotic, hare-brained—"

Wow. His ditching me at the altar turned out to be the best thing that could have happened. I wouldn't have liked spending the rest of my life with such a sharp-tempered man.

He whirled back to face me. "You're lying. No one would have sold jewelry as expensive as what I gave you at a yard sale. This isn't over, Shelby."

"Drop dead." I planted my gloved hands on my hips. "Whatever we had is over and done with. I've moved on and you're doing the same."

He glared, then stormed away.

Someone must have alerted Heath because he rushed toward us. "Is everything all right?" He put a hand on my shoulder and glanced to where Donald had stormed away.

"It's wonderful." I smiled and waved a hand toward the onlookers. "I'm closing a chapter of my life for good. All you looky-loos can go away now. The show is over."

The crowd dispersed.

"My ex is getting remarried and wanted some of the things he'd given me back. I told him I sold them."

"I remember. He had given you a lot of jewelry." Pain clouded his eyes. "I'll never be able to give you that, Shelby."

"Maybe not, but you love me and only me. I won't have to share you with other women. That is far more precious." I caressed his cheek. "Want to help me put these tools away and string Christmas lights?"

"I'd love to." The pain faded, to be replaced by a twinkle. "Obviously you plan on hanging them everywhere."

"Obviously. You can't have too many lights at Christmas."

Heath grabbed the handles of the wheelbarrow and led the way to the far corner of the community to where my garden shed and greenhouse were. "Where did you get all the poinsettia's? I've never seen so many in one place."

"I ordered them. Alice gave me a Christmas decorating budget. I spent it all on flowers and lights." I grinned and unlocked the shed door.

Once we stepped inside, Heath released the wheelbarrow and pulled me into a hug. "Want me to kiss you hard enough to make you forget that jerk of an ex?"

I wrapped my arms around his neck. "That would be wonderful."

He lowered his head and engulfed all my senses until someone cleared their throat. I lifted my head.

Donald stood in the doorway. "I forgot to give you this." He handed me a box containing a watch and money clip I'd given him. "Some of us keep the gifts."

"They're yours. I don't want them." I stepped away from Heath. A rustling sound drew my attention to the window where purple-haired Birdie ducked out of sight. Nosy woman. "I asked you to go away. There should be no reason for us to ever have to see or speak to each other again." The pain of betrayal and humiliation washed over me as it had on what would have been our wedding day.

"You heard her." Heath motioned toward the door.

Donald shook his head, grabbed the box he had given me out of my hands, and muttered something about crazy women as he marched away.

I sagged against a work bench. Why did he still affect me so? Because I thought I'd loved him. I'd given him my heart only to have it trampled on. I glanced up at Heath. Now, I had a wonderful man and I was afraid to give him the same commitment.

"Come on." He held out his hand with a smile. "Let's go string lights and turn this place as bright at night as it is during the day."

I slipped my hand in his and let him lead me to the storage shed where boxes and boxes of lights waited. I clapped my hands and ripped into the first one. "I hope we have enough."

"Sweetheart, you have more than enough." He shook his head. "You can cover every bush along the walkways."

"Don't forget the pool area. I wanted to decorate the maze, too, but I ran out of money."

"My back will be very grateful." He loaded a box onto a wheeled cart. "Alice gave me a list of repairs, but they won't take long."

"Thank you for helping me."

He winked. "I'd rather do this than fix toilets and leaky faucets."

By the time all the lights were strung, I lost count of how many strands, I barely had time to take a shower before the supper bell rang. I met up with Mom and Grandma on the way to the dining hall and flipped the switch near the door that would turn on the timer for the lights to come on at dusk.

"I heard Donald came by," Grandma said as we entered the hall. "Are you all right?"

"I'm fine. He wanted his gifts back."

"I'm not giving back the necklace I bought." She narrowed her eyes.

"There's no need to. He knows they're gone." I headed for the buffet and filled my plate with a large salad, fried chicken, and fried potatoes. I needed the sustenance after the day I'd had. Plate full I joined Heath at our usual table.

It had once been designated the employee table, but my family and friends took it over as our place to sit. The other employees sat wherever they could find an empty seat. Except for Alice Johnson, the manager. She'd integrated herself into our group.

She now approached the table, clomping on high heels she couldn't gracefully walk in, and plopped next to me. "Shelby, this community has had enough drama. Please take care of past business off campus."

"He wasn't invited." I drizzled ranch dressing over my salad. "I don't think he'll be back."

"See that he isn't. The complex is at full capacity, for once. No more deaths, thefts, or exes, please." She straightened. "Much more of that and we'll get a bad reputation."

"Pish posh," Grandma said, waving her glass of wine. "It'll draw people. We'll be known as the community of excitement."

"I'm with Alice." Ted, Grandma's boyfriend and a retired cop, sat down. "The trouble Shelby gets into is enough to make me gray haired."

"Darling." Grandma ran her finger through his thick hair. "You already are."

"See what she does?" He grinned.

Mom patted my hand in a gesture of goodwill. "You do tend to put everyone on edge, dear."

I sighed and concentrated on my food. After the last fiasco where someone was poisoning people with deadly plants from my garden, I swore off solving crime. Every time, either myself or someone I cared about came within an inch of losing their life. It wasn't that I went looking for murder and mayhem. But rather that it followed me like a homeless person to a free buffet.

Heath leaned close. "Don't listen to them."

"You agree."

"True, but I also want you to be happy."

Sweet Heath. I planted a kiss on his cheek. "Let's get through Christmas without someone dying and I'll be happy."

Seth Willis, police officer and beau of my best friend, marched to our table. "Shelby, come with me, please."

"Why? I'm eating." Seriously, the man was becoming a thorn in my side. While we were tip-toeing around friendship, he still thought me little more than a troublemaker.

"I don't want to make a scene."

"Fine." I stood, as did the rest of the table. It wasn't as if he could make an announcement for me to follow him and not have them curious.

Seth led us to a far corner near the fountain.

Birdie perched on a concrete bench, jumping to her feet when we came near. "The body is over there." She glared at me.

A body? My heart sank to my knees.

Heath grasped my hand.

Taking my strength from him, I stepped forward. A man's legs stuck out from crushed poinsettia plants. I took a deep breath and followed the legs up to the face. Donald! A string of Christmas lights were wrapped around his neck. My legs gave way and I crumpled to the ground.

Heath knelt and wrapped his arms around me.

Seth stood over us. "Do you know this man?"

"My ex-fiance." I forced the words from a throat clogged with tears.

"You were seen arguing with him earlier and quoted as saying 'drop dead'. Is this true?"

I nodded.

"You can't possibly think Shelby killed him," Heath said, his voice cold. "Don't you know her well enough by now."

"I'm taking you both in for questioning. Don't move."

"You didn't know him." I glanced at Heath's face, illuminated by multi-colored Christmas lights and looking anything but festive.

"Do something Teddy!" Grandma clutched his arm.

"There isn't anything I can do. She isn't under arrest, right Seth?"

"Just a person of interest."

This couldn't be happening. Yes, I was angry at Donald. I'd said some hateful words. But, I would never kill anyone. A sense of de ja vu washed over me. The very first murder of a resident, Maybelle, had resulted in Heath and I being suspects.

I pushed to my feet and faced Seth. "You know I'm not capable of murder." I cut a sharp glance at Birdie. "I thought we were friends. I caught Maybelle's killer."

She lowered her head. "I only said what I saw and heard."

"Right. That I wanted someone dead."

"Did you say it?" Seth asked.

"Yes, but I didn't mean it literally."

"Do I need to cuff you and Heath or will you come peaceably?"

I sighed and headed for the parking lot.

2

At least Seth didn't put us in a holding tank. Instead, Heath and I waited for him in a small room with a table and three chairs. It would have been cozy, if not for the two-way mirror taking up one wall. Who watched from the other side? Boonesville, Arkansas wasn't exactly a booming metropolis with several police officers at their disposal. At my last count, they had three. The only one I knew personally was Seth.

Wait until Cheryl heard about him dragging me to the station. She was going to give him an earful.

"It might not be good for you to wear a smug look," Heath whispered.

"Oh, right." I cleared my face of all emotion. Still, I couldn't wait until my friend got a hold of Seth.

Seth entered the room. "You're looking happy for

someone suspected of murder." He glared and took a seat across from us. "We don't normally interview suspects together, but we're shorthanded."

"You know we're innocent, so cut to the chase," Heath said, crossing his arms. "We've both been through this before."

Seth exhaled sharply. "I'm just doing my job." He opened a leather binder and pulled out a pen. "Where were you this evening around six o'clock, Shelby?"

"Eating supper in front of most of the community." Seriously? That's where he took me from.

"What time did you arrive there?"

"When the bell rang at five o'clock. I didn't have time to choke, uh, Donald, with a string of lights, then make it to the dining hall. I'm five foot two inches tall and weigh one hundred five pounds. It would have taken me a while."

"Heath?"

"I arrived there a little after five."

Seth sat back in his chair. "I know you two didn't do it, but you were the only ones handy that had a motive. Can you give me the names of those who were at the dining hall? That leaves everyone else for me to question."

"I don't know all the names of the new residents," I said. "But maybe Alice can fill in any blanks." I rattled off the names of those I'd seen, Heath added a few, and still Seth had more people to interview than made him happy.

"You're free to go." He looked so dejected I couldn't help but reach across the table and pat his hand.

"We'll catch whoever did this."

His head snapped up. "There is no 'we', Shelby."

Heath sighed. "Dude, when are you going to learn? Shelby can't help but get involved." He took me by the arm and led me from the room.

"It's personal this time," I said.

"You say that every time."

Well, it was this time. Someone I had once loved very much had died a horrible death. Despite my resolve to stay out of snooping, I couldn't stay out of this one.

We walked across the street to a small park where Heath called Ted to come and pick us up. While we waited, I picked at the splintered corner of the picnic table we sat at.

Tears stung my eyes. I'd gone from loving Donald, to disliking, to apathy, and now sorrow. The man had been a two-timing skunk, more interested in notches on his belt than in commitment. Still, no one deserved to die as he had and especially during the holidays.

A pall hung over the Christmas season. One I needed to help lift.

Heath put his hand over mine. "I'm sorry about Donald."

"I don't even know where to look for his killer."

"I should tell you to leave it to the police, but I

know better. I'll help you, sweetheart. We'll question every single resident if we have to. Someone had to have seen or heard something. Call Cheryl and see if she knows the name of his fiancé. Maybe she can give us a lead."

"That's a good idea." I pulled my cell phone from the pocket of my jeans and dialed my friend.

"Oh, my gosh, Shelby. Are you all right? Sue Ellen told me Seth dragged you down to the station. Wait until I call him."

"I'm fine, and don't give Seth a hard time. He knows we're innocent. He wanted possible leads more than anything. Which, by the way, is why I'm calling. What is Donald's fiance's name?"

"Sasha Woodward. She's the art teacher here. I'm sorry I didn't tell you."

"None of my business. Can you text me her contact information?"

"You might want to question every teacher here under the age of thirty. He's been with most of them at one time or another since your split."

I closed my eyes, the pain of betrayal fresh again. "Send me their info, too."

"I'm taking vacation along with Christmas break and coming to help. I'll be there Saturday."

"No. These things I get mixed up in are too dangerous. I don't want to worry about you."

"Don't be silly. Look, one of my students stuck a permanent marker up his nose. Gotta go. See you this weekend." Click.

"See's coming to help." I folded my arms on the table and rested my head on them. Having my friends and family in harm's way was different than myself in dangerous situations. More than once, I'd found myself facing a killer. How many more times before I didn't make it out of those situations alive?

Ted and Grandma pulled up in his renovated 1957 Thunderbird. Like a diva from old Hollywood, Grandma waved a scarf. "Yoo hoo!"

I shook my head and climbed into the backseat with Heath.

Normally, we'd spend the time snuggling. This time, we sat lost in our thoughts.

Grandma chattered away, filling the silence. "Once people found out the dead guy was your ex fiancé, well, rumors and speculation filled the air." She glanced over her shoulder. "Everyone loves you, Shelby, but they also say that a jilted lover is capable of anything."

"Seth knows we're innocent," Heath said.

"Well, not everyone else believes the same." She pouted and turned back around, muttering something about ostriches with their heads in the sand.

I wasn't quite sure what she meant, but decided to leave it alone. There was enough going on in my head without worrying about her feelings being hurt.

Once Ted stopped in the parking lot, we all trooped to my cottage where Mom already waited. I glanced around for her boyfriend, Bob, but I guess we didn't have the pleasure. He tended to stay away when crime solving was involved.

"I've made coffee." Mom smiled. "I'm not going to pretend that my daughter isn't going to get involved or that we won't be up half the night coming up with a plan."

"Finally," Grandma said. "You're learning how it's done."

Mom shot her a sharp look then poured the coffee, handing us each a mug. "I'm resigned to the fact that my daughter thrives on danger and that my mother encourages her."

"There is nothing wrong with wanting my grandchild to have a more exciting life than her mother who is content to sit behind a desk and wear her hair in a bun." Grandma set her coffee aside and pulled a bottle of wine from her canary yellow bag.

"Can we please be civil to one another?" I glanced from Mom to Grandma. "Remember how your bickering almost got us eaten by a bear."

Grandma waved a hand. "That was over a month ago."

Sometimes I felt like the oldest of us three. Mom dressed like a wall flower, hair tamed back from her face. Most often she wore a cardigan over a blouse. Grandma couldn't be more different. Animal prints, bright red hair, scarlet fingernails, and the ever present bottle of wine. Me…petite with hair bigger than I was. I think God chose three random people to go through life together. The only thing we shared, physically, was blue eyes.

Ever the peacekeeper, Heath said, "I think we should focus on the task at hand."

"Agreed." Ted took the wine from Grandma. "Try coffee."

"Oh, pooh, Teddy. You know my fruit beverage helps me think clearly." She took back the bottle.

He shot me an amused glance. "I tried."

Mom handed me my fluorescent pink clipboard. "Let's get to work so we can go to bed."

"This is not something I wanted to get involved in again."

"Too late for that. You were going to marry the man. As awful of a person as he was," Grandma said, pouring wine into a glass, "he deserves justice. Now, who are the suspects besides you and Heath?"

"We aren't suspects." I groaned. Why didn't she listen to me? "Everyone who wasn't at supper is a suspect. The women he cheated with are suspects. Possibly the fiancé. She's the only one whose name we know. Sasha Woodrow."

"She sounds like a stripper," Grandma said.

Choosing to ignore her, I glanced at the others. "Who do we know that was not at supper?"

Ted pursed his lips. "Not many people turn down food that's included in their rent, but that Leroy Manning was absent."

Our neighborhood vampire, a man who was

severely allergic to the sun, never attended meals. But, he was a good one to talk to. He saw more of what went on around here than anyone. I wrote down his name and put a star.

The others rattled off names and, if they didn't know the name, a description. We were getting nowhere fast. "I really want this solved by Christmas. I do not want to spend the holidays fighting off a killer."

"No guarantees," Grandma said.

"For once, I'm on Shelby's side in this crime solving business." Mom patted my shoulder. "Let's not ruin our Lord's birthday with bloodshed. We have a little under four weeks to solve this."

I bit my lip. A nearly impossible task with no suspects. "Cheryl is coming on Saturday with information on the teachers at the school that Donald had affairs with. I'm starting my investigation with them."

"You'll have to give that list to Seth," Ted said, giving me a stern look. "He tolerates you snooping, but he won't allow you to impede his investigation."

"No problem." I knew people would rather talk to little ole me than a cop. They'd tell me things they wouldn't tell him.

I made a column on my paper for teachers and scanned the list of other names. "What motive would anyone at Shady Acres have for murdering a man they'd never met?"

"None." Heath crossed his arms. "I think we should

focus on the women he fooled around with."

"No wrath like a woman scorned and all that, right?" Grandma raised her glass in a toast.

"Right." Come Saturday, I'd be knocking on at least one person's door. My five-foot-eleven-inch best friend would be my bodyguard. Mild-mannered and not the least bit brave, it was her size that tended to steer people away from doing me harm. It had happened all through high school. "Anything else before we wrap this up?"

"There are five of us here on a regular basis. Six if you count Cheryl," Grandma said. "I think we need a club. Something cool to call ourselves. Like the Shady Acres Gumshoes. Yes, I like the name."

"You've had enough." Ted took away the bottle and the glass and handed them to Mom. "We aren't crime fighters. We don't need a club or a name."

"The newspapers need something to call us." She frowned. "So far, they've only mentioned Shelby."

"That's because I come close to being killed on a regular basis."

3

*"H*ello, everyone!" Cheryl stepped through the dining hall door at breakfast on Saturday morning.

Immediately every man with a heartbeat focused his attention on her. Tall, blond, and buxom, she usually could get them to do anything for her. Today was no exception. Four men rushed to take her suitcases.

Grandma glanced down at her chest. "I need a boob job."

Ted spewed orange juice across the white tablecloth. "Whatever for?"

"So men will do my bidding like they do her."

"Sweetheart, I'll do anything you ask, flat chested or not."

"Thank you, Teddy." She grasped his face in both hands and planted a big kiss on his lips.

I shook my head and rushed toward my friend, wrapping my arms around her. "Thank you for coming."

"Girl, the things you get into are the only excitement I get. Seth refuses to tell me about the cases he's working on." She took a seat next to me. "Where's your hunky hero?"

I shrugged. "Alice has him doing something important." I did finger quotes around the word important. "I made a list of the names you sent, but want your input on who to start questioning first."

"I can't wait to get started." She accepted full plates of food from two old men who could barely shuffle across the room. "Just as soon as I eat."

Seth marched through the door and straight to our table. "The list, Shelby."

Sighing, I forwarded him Cheryl's text. "Hello to you, too."

"Good morning, gorgeous." He ignored me and kissed Cheryl. "I'll be back for supper." And, just as fast as he arrived, he left.

"Why couldn't he just call?" I glared at his back.

"He didn't think you'd give him the list unless he told you in person."

"Why didn't you give it to him?"

Cheryl shrugged. "He didn't ask me."

Sometimes, I swore my friends and family personally tried to thwart my attempts at...anything. Why did I always have to be the one in the police department's crosshairs? "If we're going to be a team, I could use a little help with the tiny details once in a while."

"Team?" Alice joined us. "I want in."

"We're solving a murder," Grandma said. "You wouldn't be interested."

"Who says? I'm very interested in everything that goes on here." She pouted. "Oh, and Shelby, are you ready for tonight's Winter Ball?"

Yikes. Not only was I the gardener for Shady Acres, but the events coordinator as well. I'd completely forgotten about tonight's big event after Donald's demise. Questioning suspects would have to wait until tomorrow. "Except for a few minor details." Like decorations, a gown, food.

"Wonderful. Now, what about this team you're getting together?" Alice smiled.

"It's not really that. Grandma has loose lips. I'm going to solve the murder, if I can."

Alice grinned. "That's right. The dead guy is your ex-fiance."

"How do you know that?"

"Everyone knows." She rubbed her hands together. "What would you like me to do first?"

"Make a list of everyone who wasn't at that night's supper." That should keep her busy for a while.

"It'll take some work, but I can think of something." She leaped from her chair and rushed toward her office.

"Smart way to get rid of her." Grandma grinned.

"She might actually be able to help. Now, I'm off to visit the kitchen staff about food for tonight's party. Cheryl, could you find me a gown to wear?"

"You got it, toots. I'll make sure you look gorgeous. I brought something perfect for myself to wear."

I'm sure she did. I headed for the kitchen and stepped inside the marble and stainless steel room. Joyce, the head cook stirred a pot on the stove. Lori Brown, her helper, sliced bread. A new guy, tall and rail thin, peered over from where he washed dishes.

"Well, hello, Shelby." Joyce smiled, more of a grimace. We had a shaky relationship since I'd once accused her of poisoning the residents. "What can I do for you?"

"With all the excitement," my heart lurched, picturing Donald lying in the poinsettia's, "I forgot about tonight's party. It's a formal winter affair. What can we whip together for the menu?"

"You're killing me here." She turned off the burner under the pot on the stove. "I've got in a shipment of salmon. How about a seafood buffet? We can decorate the buffet with white lights and glitter."

I gave her an impulsive hug. "Perfect. Thank you."

She stood as stiff as an English guard. "You're, uh, welcome."

Now, to find Heath and work on decorations.

I located him, mumbling, in the storage room. "Hey."

He straightened. "Just the person I need. Alice has the insane desire for me to build more benches along the walking paths."

"What can I do?"

"Brighten my day." He gave a lopsided smile that almost sent my heart flopping.

"Want to work for me instead?" I returned his smile.

"Honey, I'd clean toilets for you."

I laughed. "Nothing as bad as all that. I need a place to have tonight's Winter Ball, and decorations gotten out of the shed."

"Cutting it close." He wiped his hands on the legs of his jeans. "I have some garden heaters. Let's use the decorations we already have. Why not have the party in the courtyard by the fountain? We already have plants and lights. Keep it simple and elegant."

"Maybe you should be the events coordinator. That's a perfect idea." I slipped my arm in his. "Let's head over there and make sure everything looks good."

We strolled to the fountain. Someone had removed the crime scene tape. I groaned. "I need to find some new poinsettias."

"For tonight, take them from somewhere else. I'll bring in the furniture from the pool and other common areas. It'll be fine." He gave me a quick hug. "I didn't think about this being where Donald died when I suggested it."

"Don't worry." I blinked back traitorous tears.

Sometime soon, I was going to have to re-evaluate my feelings about Donald's death and grief. "It will be good for something fun to happen here." Although, the fountain area was the second time a crime had occurred there, it wasn't the fountain's fault.

~

Dressed in an ice blue gown, faux fur stole around my shoulders, and my hair up, with rhinestone barrettes, I surveyed the magic of the courtyard. Heath had out done himself.

He'd turned off the multi-colored lights, leaving only the white ones and had somehow found fake snow to scatter around the ground. Glitter winked from the flakes. The buffet table sparkled with crystal and white dishes. Garden heaters kept the area a comfortable temperature. It was all beautiful and magical.

"Wow, Shelby." Alice stood next to me in a black gown. "You've outdone yourself."

"I had help, and thank you. This will really kick off the holiday season."

"You can't even tell a murder had happened here."

Gee, thanks for the reminder. My smile faded, and I wandered over to survey the seafood on ice. I'd have to thank Joyce. It couldn't have been easy to put this together on such short notice.

"You did good, girlfriend." Cheryl, accompanied by Seth, approached me.

"So did you. I feel like Cinderella in this gown."

"It's one of your grandmother's." She smiled. "Who

knows how old it is. That woman must have kept every gown from the 1920s."

I laughed. "She isn't *that* old."

Cheryl waved away my comment. "You get my meaning. The woman hoards clothes. Now, let's mingle and see whether anyone saw something they didn't know they saw the night Donald died."

"Let me handle this," Seth said.

"Nope. These old men will talk to me. You stay in the background and look handsome." She tugged the neckline of her gown a little lower and sailed away.

Seth chuckled and grabbed a plate. "Can I get my food and then do as Cheryl said? I think it wise for me to be as invisible as possible."

"Definitely. You can see everything from the shadows by those hedges." I pointed to our right. "I'll mingle, too, and play the sad jilted ex-love."

"Have you considered getting a private investigator's license?" He moved away.

Hmm. Would I have to go to school? Take a test? Learn to shoot a gun? I was kind of happy just being a nosy nobody.

"You're the most beautiful woman I've ever seen." Heath wrapped his arms around my waist from the back and nuzzled my neck.

Flushed, I turned in his arms. "You'll mess up my hair and makeup, but go ahead and kiss me."

He obliged, leaving me warmer than the heaters could do. When he pulled back, he asked, "What's Seth doing in the bushes?"

"Spying on the residents and Cheryl who is wearing a very low cut gown in order to get the old men to tell their secrets." I led him to the entrance of the courtyard. "Greet the guests with me."

We smiled as one-by-one the residents of Shady Acres entered the courtyard. If one more of them said how sorry they were for my loss, I was going to scream.

"I need to talk to you," Leroy said, stopping in front of me.

"About the night Donald was murdered?" I lowered my voice.

He nodded. "Meet me at the far corner once you've finished saying hello to all these…nosy people."

I nodded and squeezed Heath's hand. "I knew he could help us. The man doesn't miss a thing."

"Make sure Seth is close enough to hear what Leroy says. I'll go tell him to find a hiding place over there."

Keeping a smile plastered on my face, I couldn't help but wonder where Alice was. As manager, it was her job to greet folks at our events. The last time she failed to show almost resulted in her death. I pulled my cell phone from a hidden pocket in my stole and texted her.

Where are you?

Snooping. Be right there.

Snooping what?

I said I'll be right there. Geez.

Fine. I put my phone away and kept my gaze

trained on the path leading to the main building. Sure enough, Alice trotted toward me.

Grabbing my arm, she pulled me to the side. "Sorry I ditched you, but once I arrived here, I realized I didn't have my list." She handed me a folded sheet of paper. "The people who didn't show up for supper the other night."

"Thanks. Can you take over as hostess now? I need to talk to someone." Without waiting for her answer, I hurried to where Leroy waited.

He grabbed my arm and pulled me into the bushes where we collided with Seth. Leroy exhaled sharply. "I should have known the cops would be here."

"You have something to say you don't want me to hear?" Seth crossed his arms.

"I don't like people. Only Shelby."

"Thanks, Leroy. I like you, too." I smiled.

"Stop with the niceties. What do you want to tell her?" Seth's eyes glittered.

"Fine. I was taking my nightly stroll the night that man was killed. He was arguing with a woman. A woman in a black cloak. Very theatrical, don't you think?" Leroy wiggled his eyebrows.

"Get on with it," Seth ordered.

"Whatever you say, boss. So, hearing the raised voices, I crept closer," he lowered his voice. "The woman said she was tired of playing second fiddle. That he needed to stop fooling around and choose already. He begged her to be reasonable. Before I knew what was happening, she'd picked up a big rock and bashed him in the head with it." He glanced at Seth. "I bet that isn't common knowledge, is it? That he was hit in the head?"

Seth shook his head.

"Then, she grabbed a string of lights from one of the bushes and strangled him."

"Did you get a look at her face?" Seth asked.

"No, but just as I stepped on a twig, which cracked like a firecracker, she ran off. Her hood fell revealing a very lovely head covered with blond hair."

4

"*B*lond?" Cheryl's eyebrows rose. "Every woman Donald had an affair with is blond. His fiancé is blond. There's speculation as to whether she's a true blond, but…well, you get the idea."

"Then our suspect list got knocked down to four." Of course, more tended to come along as an investigation got underway, but at least we had a place to start.

Seth shook Leroy's hand. "You've given us our best lead. Thank you for your help." Then, he turned to Cheryl. "Is it at all possible for me to work without you showing up?"

She grinned. "No. I'm as nosy as Shelby."

With a groan, he marched down the pathway and back to the party.

"What did you two do to Seth?" Heath asked when

we followed. "He tossed back a tumbler of whiskey like it was water."

"I think he's realizing he can't win against us," I said, smiling.

"Poor guy." Heath put an arm around my shoulder. "Want to dance? Bob brought his record player and band music and crooner vinyls."

"That sounds lovely."

He swung me onto the dance floor to the tune of Frank Sinatra. I breathed deep of his cologne, closed my eyes, and leaned my head on his chest. It surprised me how safe I felt with Heath after only a few months. After Donald, I thought I'd never love again. I prayed Heath would be patient enough to wait until I could say the words.

After two songs, he led me to the buffet. "Let's eat. I can hear your stomach growling over the music."

"Mine or yours?" I grabbed a plate and handed him one.

"Okay, mine." He grinned and grabbed a slice of salmon with mango salsa. "I think this is the best meal the chef has put together yet. Great music, beautiful atmosphere, good food, and a gorgeous date. What more could a man ask for?"

"Not to be plagued by crazy women?" I pointed to where a beautiful blond woman in black leggings and a baggy sweatshirt stood next to the fountain.

She put her fingers to her lips and blew a piercing whistle until everyone else stopped and looked her way.

"I want to talk to Shelby Hart."

"That's me." I handed my plate to Heath, then stepped forward.

Cheryl grabbed my arm. "I'm coming with you. That's Sasha, and she's nuts."

I sure wished I could have one night with Heath that wasn't shadowed by drama or death. With my heart in my throat, I approached the crazy-eyed woman. "Let's step over here where we can talk in private." I led her to the other side of the fountain. Heath and Seth could still see us, but we weren't in full view for all the gawkers.

Sasha's brown eyes were red-rimmed. Smudged mascara gave them a hollowed out look. Even distraught, the woman was drop dead gorgeous. "You were once engaged to my Donald, right?"

I nodded. "But, he ditched me on our wedding day for someone else."

"Who? I demand to know." She gripped my arm and gave me a shake.

"Hands off, lady." Cheryl pushed her back.

"What's the Amazon going to do about it?" Sasha glared. "I want to speak to every cheating, wanton, woman that kept my Donald from giving me his whole heart."

Was this woman for real? "Do you have proof he cheated on you?"

She threw a cell phone at me. "It's full of women's phone numbers!"

"Look, Sasha. You're upset. Go home and sleep it

off. Why dwell on the bad? The man you love is dead." I picked up the phone from where it had fallen next to the path and returned it to her. "Wait a few days and talk to these women reasonably. I'm sure you'll all have a lot of things to say to each other."

She tilted her head. "Wasn't he with you on the day he died?"

"Yes, but only to ask me to give back the jewelry he gave me so he could give it to you. I'm sorry to tell you I sold it all."

"He really meant nothing else to you?"

"I promise. Do you need someone to give you a ride home?"

She shook her head. "I haven't been drinking, just crying." She turned and shuffled down the walkway.

"I told you she was nuts." Cheryl crossed her arms.

"She's grieving. Let her be." I returned to Heath and my food. "Everything is fine." Not really. More than one woman would shed tears over Donald, myself included.

"Did she tell you anything I need to know?" Seth asked.

"No." I sat at one of the bistro-style tables. "You should probably keep an eye on the women on that list I gave you, though. Sasha plans on confronting each of them. She might be a bit unstable."

"Is she fine with you?" Heath sat next to me.

"I think so." I cut into my salmon. My appetite wasn't there, but I refused to let good food go to waste because a stranger showed up at a party. Still, my heart ached for her. I could, in a sense, empathize with her.

By the time the ball broke up at midnight, I was as exhausted mentally as I was physically. Back at my cottage, I hung up Grandma's dress and crawled into bed without putting on my pajamas. I lay on my back, tears trickling down my cheeks, and stared through the dark at the ceiling. Tonight, and tonight only, I would shed tears for what could have been. In the morning, whatever I once felt for Donald would be put away and the search for his killer would start in earnest.

~

The next morning I chose a simple breakfast of coffee and toast with Cheryl for company. "Who should we start questioning first?"

"I have a map." She spread a map of the city on the table. "We'll start with the closest and work away or vice versa. I'm leaving Sasha on the list. We need to talk to her away from here. She might know something if asked the right questions."

"Any idea who Seth is starting with?" I leaned over the map.

"I wish. We could start opposite him and get the facts first."

I glanced up. "We're helping, not impeding."

"Yeah, right." She grinned and sipped her coffee. "We need to get a move on if we want to sneak out without your grandmother."

"True." I stood and grabbed my purse. "We'll go

the long way to the parking lot. Maybe she won't see us." I loved the woman, but sometimes she was more trouble than help. Especially during an interview of a suspect.

Like fugitives, we bolted out the door and around my garden shed to the parking lot. Grandma leaned against my Volkswagon, arms and ankles crossed.

"I was beginning to think you two ditched me."

"We didn't tell you when we were leaving." I pressed the car fob to unlock the doors. "Let me and Cheryl do the talking."

"Of course. I always sit and keep my mouth shut. I'm there to observe and notice." She slid into the back seat.

I rolled my eyes and climbed into the driver's seat. "I'm serious, Grandma. Don't mess this up or we won't bring you again."

"I have no idea what you're talking about."

I inserted the key and drove to the freeway. "Punch the first address into your GPS, Cheryl. You're the one guiding us."

"Gotcha."

We drove to the home of April Marks, a first grade teacher at Cooper Elementary. I remembered her from my days of teaching. A small, petite, curvy blond with an infectious smile. Don't let her looks deceive you, though. The woman could be as mean as a badger when provoked.

We stopped in front of a bungalow style home

painted a cheery yellow with a white door and shutters. "Ugh," Cheryl said, "the house is as cute as she is."

"Stop it." I climbed out and headed for the front door, leaving the others to follow. We had four women to visit that day and couldn't waste any time. I rang the doorbell and stepped back to wait.

Within a few minutes, a sleepy April answered the door. "Shelby? What in the world are you doing here?"

"I'd like to talk, if that's all right."

She narrowed her eyes. "Is this about Donald? I may have been the one who broke up your wedding, but he left me for someone else."

Well, that was one question answered. "It's not about that. May we come in?"

She peered around me at the other two. "I don't like Cheryl. She scares me."

"She'll be on her best behavior. Please."

"All right." She opened the door and ushered us inside. "At least you aren't sending me text after text like his latest fiancé. That woman doesn't give up."

I glanced around the tropical themed room. "What does she want?"

"The same thing you do. To talk." She motioned for us to sit on the wicker sofa. "What do you want to ask me?"

"When was the last time you spoke to Donald?"

"At work on the day he died." She lowered her head. "He wanted back a necklace he had given me. I told him I'd give it to him the next day, but it was too late."

So, he was gathering up all of his gifts for Sasha. Interesting. "Did you argue?"

"No."

Cheryl snorted. "Everyone heard you screeching about him being an Indian giver. Not politically correct, by the way."

"Well, he was. He gave me that necklace. Donald was a horrible lying cheat and he got what he deserved, God rest his soul. Would y'all like some tea?"

"We would not." Grandma twisted her lips between her fingers, trying desperately to hold back her words…and failed. "That was a mean and cruel thing to say about a dead man. A man killed in a vicious, twisted way. Maybe you killed him."

"Me?" April put a hand to her chest. "The man was a foot taller than me."

"He was found near a bench," I added. "Maybe you stood on that bench and wrapped the lights around his neck."

"Oh, please. You should be a fiction writer, Shelby." She crossed her legs. "Regardless of what I said, I loved Donald. We all did. Every stupid woman that got involved with him."

"One of you killed him," I said, taking note of the crossing and now uncrossing of her legs.

"It wasn't me. So, if you're going to ask me the same questions over and over, you should leave. I have lesson plans to make."

"Do you own a black cloak?" Cheryl asked.

"Yes." April frowned. "Why?"

"Just wondering." She stood. "We're done here. Oh, and the police will be by soon to ask you more questions. If you think of anything you forgot to tell us, here's my number." She scribbled it on the back of an envelope from the coffee table.

When she went to hand it to April, I caught side of something written on the other side. The address to Shady Acres. "Have you ever been to the place Donald was killed?"

"That place full of old people? No."

"Then why do you have the address written down?"

"Oh, that. Because, well, I'm looking for a place to put my grandmother."

"You don't put grandparents somewhere, Miss," Grandma said, scowling. "You help us. My money is on you, little girl. I'll prove it, too."

"Whatever." April tossed her head. "You can go now. I'm getting upset."

I sighed and glared at Grandma, before forcing a smile on April. "Thank you. Please do call if you think of anything. I'd like to find out what happened to Donald."

"Why?" Bright spots of red glowed on her cheeks. "The world is rid of one more philanderer. You ought to give flowers to the killer."

5

"She's a definite suspect," Cheryl said as we headed back to my car.

I nodded, figuring the other women on our list would dislike Donald as much as April. "Who's next?"

"Michelle Boudreau. She's...exotic looking. She's new to the school." Cheryl settled back in her seat. "You never had to worry about Donald with me."

"Because you're my best friend, right?" I cut her a sideways glance. "Or, are you comparing yourself to these women?"

"Both."

"Seriously? You're tall, blond, beautiful, and have majestic boobs. Of course Donald cast you several lustful glances." I'd elbowed him a few times for them.

She grinned. "Really?"

"Really. I'm the one who doesn't the fit the profile." Surprisingly, that no longer bothered me very much.

"Nope. You're the type every man wants to take home to Mom. Gorgeous, stylish, and well-mannered. No wonder Heath fell fast and hard."

"He did, didn't he?" I smiled and parked in front of a two-story Victorian. How could a teacher afford a place like this?

As if she could read my mind "Cheryl said, "There's speculation Michelle has a *night* job." She made finger quotes. "But no one can prove it. Another rumor is that she inherited."

I shrugged and opened the car door. How she came about her money was none of our business. "Let's get this over with."

I walked up the porch steps and rang the doorbell next to the navy blue door. I'd almost given her up as to not being home when the door opened and I stared into a pair of almond shaped, almost black, eyes. Even without makeup Michelle could grace the cover of Cosmo.

"If you're selling, I'm not buying."

"I'm not. My name is—"

She looked past me to Cheryl. "If I would have seen you, I wouldn't have answered the door."

Cheryl laughed. "Why do you think I hid behind the pillar?"

"Focus," I hissed. "Michelle, I used to be engaged

to Donald Trayer and—"

Her lips curled, "So, you're the one who couldn't hold onto her man." She peered around me at Grandma who said she would stay outside and stand guard. From whom, I had no idea, but it left me free to question people without her interfering.

I bit back a groan. "Yes, that would be me. May we ask you a few questions?" Five minutes after meeting her and I despised the woman.

"Sure, I'm not doing anything. I'll tell you whatever you want to know about the weasel." She stepped aside and ushered us into a home that either Michelle was very talented in home décor, or she had hired an interior designer.

A small Christmas tree sat on top of an end table. All the bulbs and lights were white and silver. Even the tree skirt sported silver stars. The tree was the only tribute to Christmas I saw. The rest of the furniture was done in muted tones of salmon and sand color. Very modern.

"Want a coke?" Michelle raised her eyebrows.

We shook our heads. "No, just a few questions and we'll be out of your hair," I said.

"Have a seat."

We both perched on the edge of the sofa.

"Have the police been by yet?" I asked, trying to get comfortable on the hard cushion.

"Last night a good looking one came by. Unfortunately, he had the personality of a porcupine."

Cheryl bristled next to me.

I put a hand on her leg to settle her. "Since I knew Donald, I'm trying to find out a bit of how he died. Would you mind telling me where you were on the night he was killed?"

"Having dinner with a man. No, I cannot give you his name. Our relationship is complicated."

He was married, she meant. I'd bet my car. "Any idea who might have killed him?"

She studied her sculpted nails. "Any female, I reckon. Oh, sure, we all fell for him at first, but then he showed his true colors. You should know that better than anyone." She speared me with a glance. "Maybe you killed him. You had a strong enough motive. Or, you had your giant freak here do the deed. I doubt you were strong enough, come to think of it."

"I'm stronger than I look." We were getting nowhere fast.

She gave a sly smile. "The other castoffs have formed a club. The Second Mistress Club. Not very original, I know, but you're welcome to join. We're meeting Friday night at Betty's Bar. Seven o'clock. That wimpy Sasha will be there, too. I have no idea why April invited her, but it's too late now. You can do your detecting then while we're all in one place. Cheryl is *not* invited."

I took that as a dismissal and stood. "I guess that's all. Thank you for your time."

"No problem. Good luck." She laughed, letting us

see ourselves out.

"You aren't seriously thinking about going to their little get together are you?" Cheryl asked the moment we stepped outside. "You'll be a mouse among cats."

"I think I've proven I can handle myself in tough situations." I slid back into the driver's seat. "Jeanna next, right?"

I remembered her from my teaching days. A little older, but a whole lot looser than the other women. At least outwardly. Still, we'd gotten along all right for a while. Then, she'd stopped talking to me altogether.

"She lives in Boonesville Vista Resort. In other words, the trailer park."

"Has she always lived there?" The woman was pretty and athletic, but I couldn't see Donald interested in her. He seemed too big of a snob to date someone in a trailer park.

"No, she went bankrupt a few months ago. Lost everything. If you want to meet someone who really hates Donald, it's her." Cheryl shook her head. "Maybe you can find out why. She doesn't like you much either. Did you know you're the one Donald left her for?"

I snapped around to look at her. "Then why are we visiting her?"

"Because, the rumor mill has it that he got back with her right after leaving Michelle. It was Jeanna, you, Michelle, Jeanna, April, and then Sasha. I never could figure out why he dated Jeanna twice."

I raised my eyebrows. A very good point. I pulled in

the entrance of the trailer park and parked beside a single wide near the back.

Rust dotted the corners of Jeanna's home. No grass or flowers grew anywhere close by. I actually felt sorry for her demise, now that I knew why she didn't like me. Still, we had something in common. Maybe I could use that to get her to cooperate.

I glanced in the rearview mirror as a vehicle pulled behind us. "Uh-oh. Seth is here."

He got out of his squad car and knocked on my window.

With a sigh, I rolled it down. "Hey."

"What are you doing here?"

"Looking for Jeanna." I hated the mirrored sunglasses he wore.

"Questioning her?"

"Don't ask questions you don't want the answer to," Cheryl said. "You know exactly what we're doing. Besides, Shelby got invited to a club these women belong to. We're only looking to get more information about that before she commits."

Oh, good thinking. I smiled. "Considering one of these women might be a murderer, it's wise, don't you think?"

His face gave away no sign of what he thought or felt. After an interminable long few seconds, he gave a curt nod. "Getting inside like that might actually help us."

"So, can we go in now?"

"She isn't home. Either that, or she isn't answering the door."

"She won't while you're parked there either," Cheryl said. "Go away. We'll see you back at Shady Acres in an hour. Shelby, park in front of a different trailer and we'll wait."

I eased forward the moment Seth stepped back. "You sure do know how to handle him."

"He likes when a woman takes charge."

"Sure he does." I laughed.

"Well, not really, but we'll argue a little when we get together, and then we'll make up. That's why I boss him around. The making up is great." She wiggled her eyebrows.

"Eew." I kept an eye on my rearview mirror, hoping Jeanna would make an appearance soon.

Half an hour later, a Toyota truck that had seen better days pulled under the awning of trailer number eleven. "Text Seth and tell him we'll be late." I shoved open my door and hurried toward Jeanna, followed by a texting Cheryl, and a suspiciously silent Grandma. Cheryl ran into me, almost knocking me off my feet, when I stopped. I glared over my shoulder.

"Sorry," she mumbled.

"Come on in," Jeanna said, frowning. "Michelle told me you were making the rounds."

There went the element of surprise. We followed her into a worn, but immaculate mobile home.

"It isn't much, but it's home. Sit. I've fresh

lemonade." Without waiting for consent, she poured four glasses and handed us each one before sitting across from us. "No, I did not kill Donald. Am I sad he's dead? Absolutely not. Where was I on that wonderful evening? Here, watching TV and doing lesson plans. No alibi." She smiled over the rim of her glass. Her eyes cold and hard.

"You can see what I've fallen, to. Donald took all the gifts he had once bought me and given them to you, dear, sweet Shelby." She tilted her head. "Have they been passed on to another?"

"I sold them. He did come for them on the day he died."

She laughed without mirth. "That is priceless. Poor, financially broke, Donald. Did you know his money was gone? Flittered away like butterflies on butterflies. Now, I'm living in this dump and he's relaxing in the morgue."

"Not exactly relaxing." I frowned and sat my untouched drink on the coffee table. I wasn't thirsty enough to drink anything this crazy woman handed me. "Someone killed him."

She cocked her head. "And you want to know if it was me." She exhaled heavily. "If only I'd thought of it. What restitution!"

"It wouldn't have brought you money."

Her eyes widened. "No? I guess you haven't heard. Dear Donald left money to all of us in his will. Even you. Once his assets are liquidated, we'll each have a hundred thousand dollars."

"You said he was broke."

"He is broke, cash wise. Everything is tied up in real estate. He may have been the principal of an elementary school, but his parents were loaded, until Donald got his hands on the family fortune. All that's left to do now, is for his lawyer to sell off everything." She smiled. "Any plans for your share?"

"You're getting money, Shelby." Grandma clutched my hand.

I didn't want a cent of it. "Charity, I guess."

"Still the sweet little Shelby despite everything you've been through. How quaint. If only there were more of you in the world."

"We didn't come here so you could belittle Shelby," Cheryl said, setting her glass down with a thunk. "We came to catch a killer. My eye is on you."

"Oh, I'm so scared."

"We're all victims here, Jeanna," I said, standing. "You aren't the only one Donald hurt. Instead of bashing each other, we should work together to find out who killed him."

"You go right ahead. You seem to have a knack for that sort of thing. Me? Well, I'll sit back and wait to get my share of his money. It's small compensation for the humiliation, but it's something." She tossed her long blond ponytail over her shoulder. "I was the first. That makes it that much more degrading."

I stared at the broken woman in front of me for a

minute, taking note of the flicker of pain in her eyes, then turned to leave. "I'm sorry for your loss. It's obvious you still care a great deal for him."

A long line of cursing followed us out to the car.

"Wow. That woman is definitely capable of murder." Grandma cast a look over the roof of the car. "We're lucky she didn't poison our drinks."

"You drank the lemonade?" My mouth dropped. After all the poisonings during the last murder she would take something from a suspect?

"Sure." She winked and got in the car. "It was good."

6

*T*he next morning, after several hours of raking leaves, I headed for my favorite thinking spot in the maze. It hadn't always been my favorite. Not when a killer had chased me through the tall hedges a few months back. But, that was behind me now and I enjoyed the quiet and beauty of the gazebo in the center.

After a day spent with desperately unhappy women, I needed solitude. Plus, I knew Seth would be hunting for me to see whether I had learned something about Donald's death that he hadn't.

I lay on my back on the wooden bench and stared up through the slats toward the late afternoon sky. In the distance, the bell signaling supper rang. I'd grab something in my cottage. The peace of my surroundings outweighed the need to eat.

I closed my eyes and let my mind sift through the day's events. Not one of the women Cheryl and I had visited seemed to hold a smidgeon of fondness for Donald. Except…Jeanna. Unless I was wrong, she still loved him despite his faults. Did she love him enough to kill him? Perhaps. They were all equal suspects in my book.

A heavy footfall sounded to my right. A twig snapped.

I bolted to a sitting position and peered down the darkening paths. Biting back the urge to say "hello" as so many stupid heroines did in horror movies, I leaped from the gazebo and raced back toward the cottages.

"Whoa." Heath grabbed me and pulled me to a stop.

I smacked his chest. "You scared me half to death."

He gave a crooked smile. "What are you doing out here alone close to dark? After checking your cottage, I knew I'd find you here."

"Worried?"

"Yes." He took my hand. "After the last few months, I don't take any chances with you. Seth is fit to be tied, convinced you've been killed and your body hidden because you don't know when to mind your own business."

As we walked home, our entwined hands swung back and forth. "I've been avoiding him, trying to wrap my head around the women I spoke to today. So much hate flowed through the day."

"Let's go to the movies so you can get away from it

all." Heath squeezed my hand.

"A date?"

"Yeah." He smiled. "Maybe dinner, too, since you skipped."

"That sounds wonderful."

We grabbed burgers, then went to the drive in to watch an action flick. We even managed to squeeze in some kissing. By the time I fell into bed after midnight, nothing filled my mind but how blessed I was to have a man like Heath by my side.

A loud knocking on the door woke me the next morning. I shuffled to the door and opened it to find a scowling Seth on my doorstep.

"I get the feeling you're avoiding me," he said. "I brought coffee." He held a tray containing three cups. "Is Cheryl here?"

"Sleeping." I waved for him to come in.

"No, I'm awake." She pulled her hair back into a ponytail as she entered the living room. "Ah, a man after my own heart."

After grilling us about where we were last night, me out with Heath, and Cheryl shopping with Mom, Seth pulled out his ever-present notepad. "Now, what did you learn yesterday from our suspects?"

"They all hated Donald," Cheryl said with a grin. "And they've formed a club."

"I already know that."

"That's pretty much it," I added. "Until the club meeting, I doubt I'll learn anything new. Although, I suspect Jeanna still has feelings for the man."

"Why do you say that?"

"It's just a feeling." I sipped my coffee. "I think any one of them are capable of murder if provoked enough."

"Have the meeting here. I want to eavesdrop through the window."

I looked at him as if he'd grown another head. "Not the first time I'm invited, Seth. Maybe the next time. I'm not thrilled to have any of them know where I live."

"It wouldn't be hard for them to find out. Your name is on the mailbox."

True. I sighed and focused on caffeine.

"We'll tell you everything we find out." Cheryl patted his hand.

"You weren't invited." I looked up. "I can't attend the first meeting with you in tow when one of the women definitely doesn't like you. Besides, the club is for Donald rejects."

"Sasha is going." She frowned. "She wasn't a reject. I can always say we dated. No one would know otherwise. We could have been discreet."

"I agree with Cheryl," Seth said. "I don't like you going into the lion's den alone."

I shook my head. "I go alone or not at all."

"Fine," they said in unison.

I went to my room and quickly tugged on a pair of faded jeans and a long sleeved blue flannel shirt before rejoining the others.

"Now that that's settled, let's go eat." I stood and stared at them until they followed.

Breakfast was uneventful, thankfully. Full of egg and bacon croissant, I went outside and climbed into my golf cart to make my rounds around the grounds. The fountain beckoned like a beacon.

The early morning sun glinted off the water pouring from the stone maiden's urn. I parked and slid out. No crime scene tape fluttered around my poinsettias, it had been taken down before the Winter Ball. One of the red flowered plants didn't take to the dirt like the others. I knelt to repack the dirt around its roots, hoping an extra dose of vitamins later would revive the plant.

As I planted my palms on my knees to stand, I noticed something shiny partially under a rock I'd dislodged with my foot. A pearl button. I used a fallen petal to pick it up. Definitely a button off a piece of woman's clothing. A clue? I hoped so, although I knew the chances of finding the item the button had fallen from would be near impossible. Still, the owner might have replaced the button and wear the item again. I slipped the button in my pocket and climbed back into my cart.

"Shelby!"

I turned to see Alice tottering toward me. "You need to stop wearing heels." I clamped a hand over my mouth. It was time someone told her, but I wasn't sure it should be me.

"Why?" She planted her fists on her hips. "They

make my legs look nice."

"But…you aren't very…graceful in them." I wanted to say those words since the moment I met her.

She narrowed her eyes. "Of course, I am. I'm a lady."

"Maybe you should wear kitten heels instead of stilettos." I smiled. "Can I do something for you?"

"Rather than insult me, you mean? Yes. I need a ride to the maze."

"Hop in. What's going on in the maze?"

"I really liked the last time you had a party there and thought we could do a magical Christmas treasure hunt. Your ideas are starting to get a little mundane. Our events need livening up."

Gee, thanks. "I'm always open to suggestions. If we did our events once a month instead of every weekend, they'd be better."

"That might not be a bad idea since all units are now rented. Let's do this last Christmas one and we'll go month-to-month. I want to hide gifts around the maze for people to find. It'll be expensive, but fun, don't you think? I like it much better than a simple gift exchange. Of course, we'll have consolation prizes."

Of course. We wouldn't want anyone to feel left out. "Instead of a treasure hunt, which we've done, why not a Christmas carnival with booth games? We could still use the maze as one of the games."

"That's an excellent idea. Why, we could have a kissing booth. The old ladies would pay a pretty penny to kiss Heath." She cut me a sideways glance. "I'll let him know it was your idea."

"That particular game wasn't." I increased our speed to where she had to grab the handle bar above her head. "If you're going to charge for the games, you need to have a reason. What will the funds be used for?"

"Purchasing gifts for under-privileged children."

That was an idea I could get behind. "Even easier would be a Christmas tree in the dining hall with the names of these children and what they need. Then, we could have a gift-wrapping party with refreshments."

"You just don't want a bunch of women kissing Heath."

True, no matter how old they were. "I'm thinking of the cost."

She sat silent for a few minutes. "Turn around. I like that idea better."

I grinned and headed toward the main building. The ugly green dragon of jealousy slid back into its burrow. I knew I shouldn't be worried about women over the age of sixty purchasing a kiss from my boyfriend, but with all the hatefulness going around, I couldn't help feeling that way. In a few weeks, I might think differently. Maybe in the spring we could do the carnival. Something like that would take a lot of planning.

I dropped Alice off and headed for the greenhouse. Inside, I checked the herbs which would no longer grow outside because of the cooling temperatures and hung some upside down to dry. Others, I placed on a towel and carried to the kitchen for Joyce to use in her cooking.

"Good morning," I sang as I entered.

"What's so good about it?" Joyce slammed a pot on the stove. "My new helper scorched the potato soup I was preparing for lunch."

"Sandwiches?"

"I suppose." She sighed. "Why is good help so hard to find?"

"I have no idea." I gave her what I hoped was a reassuring smile. "Where are Lori and Steve?"

"Inventoring the pantry. Even they can't mess that up, I hope." She wiped her hands on her apron. "Oh, nice. Fresh herbs." She took them from me and placed them on the cutting board. "I'll make baked chicken with a pesto sauce for supper. You're a good gardener, Shelby."

"Thank you. Has anyone said otherwise?"

She shrugged. "Just murmurings about how death follows you. A bunch of hogwash. Don't worry your head."

I leaned against the counter. "It does seem to follow me, though. Hardly a month goes by without someone dying by nefarious means."

"It's a curse." She waved a knife at me. "It has nothing to do with you. It's this place. Someone built a wonderful community, filled it with people from all walks of life, and voila! Murder and mayhem. You do a good job catching the bad guys, even if you do get confused sometimes. I still can't believe you thought I was poisoning people."

"I am sorry about that."

She waved away my comment. "It did make sense. I had the means, if not the motive. You be careful, Shelby Hart. You won't always be lucky. You need God on your side."

"I didn't know you were a Christian."

"Well, there's a lot people don't know about me on account of my bad temper. Think about it, Shelby, and keep your nose where it belongs."

"Thanks. I'll do my best." I'd been told that more times than I could count, yet couldn't seem to tear myself away from a new mystery.

"Sorry to hear about your ex."

"Thank you, but we were over a while ago."

"I guess you're on the hunt again, right?"

I nodded.

"I'll be praying, and I'll get the prayer chain at church active, too. God's word says He looks out for the foolish. Only He knows why. Don't be a fool and press your luck."

7

I smoothed the skirt of the simple sheath dress I wore, squared my shoulders, and entered the reserved room at the restaurant. Four heads turned to stare.

"You came," Michelle said. "I wasn't sure you would."

"I'm never one to turn down a party." I forced a smile and took the vacant seat next to Jeanna. "Besides, we all have something in common."

"Not me." Sasha sniffed and examined her nails. Several scratches marred her right hand. "I wasn't ditched. Death took Donald from me, not another woman."

"You took him from me!" April slammed her glass down. "Or was it Jeanna? I can't remember."

"Let's not squabble." Jeanna sighed. "We're here in

remembrance."

"I thought we were here to bash a dead guy." Michelle smirked.

"Why are we here, exactly?" I picked up the menu.

"Camaraderie," April said. "Isn't that a hoot? Except for Jeanna and Sasha, the rest of us can't stand the guy."

"But, we all used to love him," I added. The words tasted bitter in my throat. But, if I wanted to get the other ladies to talk freely, I'd have to encourage them. I really hoped the evening wasn't a waste of time and one of them moved up the suspect ladder.

The waitress arrived to take our order. After the others all ordered salads, I changed my mind from chicken fried steak with gravy to a salad. Groaning inwardly, I handed over my menu.

"You don't fit," Sasha said, tilting her head. "You aren't a blond. What did Donald see in you? You're tiny, skinny, and have uncontrollable hair."

I shrugged. "I was told I was the type he wanted to take home to his mother." God, forgive me, but I enjoyed the stunned expressions on their faces. These women put cattiness to a whole new level. I refused to allow them to get to me.

"The kitten has claws," Michelle said, clapping.

Sasha grabbed her purse. "I cannot believe I'm sitting here listening to this. Of course, Donald loved me. We were engaged!" She waved around her ring.

"Doesn't mean anything, toots." Michelle seemed to

be enjoying herself. "He was once engaged to Shelby, too. I guarantee he had someone else on the side while you wore his ring."

Sasha narrowed her eyes. "I'll kill her. Who is she?"

"I have no idea. I'm only speculating."

Interesting. Other than anger, Sasha didn't look surprised that Donald may have had another woman besides her. I decided to pay a little more attention to the grieving fiancé. "What happened to your hand, Sasha?"

"Rose bush. That's a passion."

Hmm. I noticed she didn't say her passion. I'd recently read somewhere that if a person doesn't 'own' their words with me, my, or I, they're most likely lying. "As a gardener, I know firsthand how dangerous plants can be. I hope you cleaned them well. They might scar." Fingernails were worse than thorns any time.

"I wish I would have killed him," Jeanna whispered. She gasped and straightened, then glanced around as if to determine whether anyone heard.

I pretended not to. Instead, I suddenly found the contents of my purse very interesting.

"What are you rummaging for?" Michelle leaned across the table.

"Lipstick." I pulled out a tube that had definitely seen better days.

She laughed. "You're a strange one, Shelby Hart. I wish we could be friends. We'd have a lot of fun."

I almost asked why we couldn't be friends, but the food arrived. All the skinny women dug into their salads like they hadn't eaten in a week. Myself included.

Occasionally, someone would say something nasty about the deceased or each other, but for the most part the get-together was congenial. I didn't learn a thing other than the fact that Sasha was a liar about how she hurt her hand. I needed to get the women at the scene of the crime.

"Shady Acres is having a gift-wrapping party for under-privileged children. Interested?" I peered over the rim of my water glass.

They glanced at each other, then nodded.

"I believe in giving," Michelle said. "We're all teachers and love children. Count us in. Maybe I'll meet myself a sugar daddy who will die and leave me his money."

I frowned. If they were going to prey on my friends, I would uninvite them. "This is a party and charitable event, not a nightclub."

"Lighten up. Just making conversation." Michelle tossed her napkin next to her plate and stood. "Well, it's not been fun, and I have things to do. Ciao." She slung her red purse over her shoulder and left.

That was our clue. The rest of us followed soon after.

I sat in my car and watched as the other women climbed into theirs. What a waste of time and unpleasant gathering. A knock on my window interrupted me.

"I don't think anyone told you," Sasha said after I rolled down my window. "Donald's funeral is tomorrow at ten a.m." She sighed and stepped back.

I nodded and started my car. This was not something I wanted to do alone. Heath would go with me for moral support without hesitation. But was it a good thing to have my current boyfriend attend the funeral of my ex?

~

"Of course, I'll go with you," Heath said in my cottage later. "I'm here for you whenever you need me."

I planted a kiss on his cheek. "You're the best. Have I told you that?"

"Not recently." He gave me a crooked smile. "How did your get-together go?"

"It was awful. To die with so many people hating you…I can't imagine."

Seth knocked, then entered. I really needed to get in the habit of locking my door.

"What did you learn?" He sat in the chair across from us.

Cheryl came down the hall and perched on the arm.

"Hello, to you, too. I didn't learn anything more than that Sasha has suspicious scratches on her right hand. She said it was from a rose bush."

He jotted down what I had said. "That's it?"

"Sorry. The funeral is tomorrow. Every one of those women are bound to be there. Oh, and I invited them to the gift wrapping party for underprivileged children. I thought they should visit the scene of the crime. The killer is bound to trip herself up."

"Crimes of passion are hard to solve," he said. "I'm not sure this was pre-meditated."

I thought for a moment. "You think the killer saw Donald talking to me and lost her mind?"

"Yes." He settled back in the chair. "I've been thinking about this case, a lot, and talking to Ted, which means your grandmother. She reminded me of the saying 'hell hath no fury like a woman scorned'. Plus, Donald was murdered with a string of Christmas lights. The killer didn't come prepared. They used what was at hand."

I agreed. The murder didn't seem planned. Since it had occurred on the same day Donald had visited requesting back his gifts, I was of the same mind as Seth. The killer had seen Donald speaking with me and acted in anger and rejection.

Heath squeezed my hand. "It wasn't your fault."

He always knew what I was thinking. I rested my head on his shoulder. "It hasn't been a very nice Christmas season so far."

"Let's change that. As soon as the funeral is over, it's all about the season, the gifts, Jesus, and family. No more murder investigating. Seth, it's all yours."

"Agreed. Shelby, you've been a big help, but this is

my job. You make sure the people here are happy. That's all you need to focus on."

"All right." I was more than happy to step aside on this one.

"Yoohoo!" Grandma and Ted waltzed into my cottage. "You young people are up late."

"Just chilling," I said, motioning for them to sit. "I'm resigning from the case."

"Oh, pooh. I was ready to get involved."

"You can come to the funeral tomorrow. Snoop to your heart's content."

She clapped. "I love funerals."

"That isn't something you should say out loud, Grandma."

"Oh, well. I have a new dress I can wear. Do you think it'll be an open casket?"

"I'm sure it will." I gave Ted an imploring look.

"I can't do a thing with her," he said. "Ida is one of a kind." He put an arm around Grandma's shoulder.

"You're so sweet." Grandma kissed him, leaving a lip print of fuchsia on his forehead.

"I'm beat. Good night." I stood and gave Heath another kiss. "Y'all can stay and chat if you want, but I'm going to bed. Lock the door when you leave."

"I'll pick you up at nine-thirty," Heath said.

I headed to bed and dreamed of angry women teachers, poinsettias, and Christmas lights.

~

The next morning, I donned a pair of black slacks

and light grey blouse. It was too cold for a dress, in my opinion. Grabbing a black trench coat from the closet, I knocked on Cheryl's door. "Ready to eat?"

"Coming." She stepped out in a navy maxi skirt and blue and black striped blouse. "I hate funerals."

"Good. You'll balance out my crazy grandmother." Huddled against a brisk wind, we rushed to the dining hall.

Alice met us at the door. "Heath will not be able to accompany you this morning. Since he did not know the deceased, I have not given him the day off. He is needed elsewhere. The kitchen sprang a huge leak and flooded my office." She raised her eyebrows as if daring me to argue.

"O...kay." I cut a sideways glance at Cheryl who made circular motions behind Alice.

"Good. He ate early and is already at work." She marched away in sensible kitten heels.

I chuckled and headed for the buffet. While she acted as if we were no longer in competition for Heath's affection, I saw the way she looked at him when she thought I wasn't. I didn't blame her. A man who looked like Chris Hemsworth would turn any woman's head. But, his outward appearance was only a bonus. It was his kindness and his heart that kept me around.

"She loves to boss you around," Cheryl said, piling a plate with eggs and bacon.

"She's the boss. That's her right." I added fruit to

my already full plate.

Cheryl groaned. "You eat as much as I do and hardly weigh as much as my right leg."

"I'm small boned, and take after my grandmother who has the metabolism of a hummingbird."

"And drinks like a fish. I bet you my next paycheck that's a mimosa she's holding in her hand."

I glanced to where Grandma sat, a wineglass in hand. "I don't know what to do about her. I mean, she's…wild. I feel as if I'm the adult here."

Cheryl laughed. "You are. I hope I'm as full of life as Ida when I'm sixty something. I asked her the other day how she stayed so active. She told me wine and chocolate."

I did love my grandmother. "Help me keep her under control at the funeral. She acts more like they're parties than a memorial service."

"I'll try not to encourage her."

We made our way to the end of the buffet, grabbed our eating utensils, and headed for the table.

"Ready to catch a killer, girls?" Grandma raised her glass in a toast. "They always show up at the funeral of their victim. This could be our day."

8

Sandwiched between Grandma and Mom, with Cheryl following, I entered the main room of the funeral home. At the front, sitting on an ornate pedestal, was an oak coffin surrounded by so many floral arrangements the air reeked. I hadn't known Donald had been so popular. The room was filled to capacity. The four of us, to Grandma's consternation, had to take seats in the back.

"You were engaged to him," Grandma said. "That should allow us to sit up front. I can't see a thing from back here."

"You can hear just fine." Mom patted her knee. "Besides, the killer always sits in the back according to the movies."

"Right." Grandma settled back and grinned, then scanned the room with narrowed eyes.

I closed my eyes and prayed Grandma would behave. Prayed. Huh. Something I seemed to be doing more and more often. Maybe heading into dangerous situations on a regular basis, as I tended to do, would restore a faith I once had.

While I knew Mom believed, she never talked about it. Grandma, on the other hand, did, but all in the name of God forgiving her for her outlandish behavior on a regular basis. Still, it was a subject I needed to visit soon. I needed healing from Donald's betrayal if I was ever going to have a future with Heath.

I took a deep breath to settle my thoughts and studied those in attendance. The jilted women and grieving Sasha were in attendance, as were many others I knew from my previous job as a teacher. A few admin from other schools, and faces I didn't recognize filled the rest of the chairs. Seth, trying to look inconspicuous in a dark suit, stood in a far corner with another man, a police officer, I assumed.

No one looked out of place.

A minister approached the podium and gave a short, but stirring message on leaving a legacy. He spoke about Donald's role in the education of our youth.

Sasha broke into loud sobs toward the end and rushed to the coffin, draping herself over the body. Her behavior seemed strange to me. I hadn't gotten the impression she was over the top in love with Donald. Sure, she cared for him, but she was as angry as the rest of them.

I gave a sad smile, noticing I didn't lump myself in with the others. I'd forgiven Donald, it seemed. After all, nearly a year was a lot of time for the cracks in a heart to fill in.

"Holding up okay?" Mom leaned close.

"I'm fine." Murder had hit closer to home this time, but I would be all right.

Heath slid into the seat next to me. "I bugged Alice until she relented." He took my hand.

Tears sprang to my eyes. I did not deserve such a caring man. "Thank you."

"You would do the same for me."

I'd like to think so. But, I wasn't sure. When his ex-fiance had shown up as an interior designer for Shady Acres, I hadn't been nearly as accommodating. I wasn't sure I could have paid my respects to a woman catty enough to try and convince me Heath couldn't be trusted.

Everyone lined up to pay their respects to the deceased. When my turn came, I glanced inside the coffin, said goodbye, and apologized for not finding his killer. Then, that chapter of my life closed and I headed to a building in back where a potluck was to be served.

Still drawn together by their common bond, the jilted ladies sat at the same table. They waved my party over. Once we sat, Seth included, all seats were taken.

Michelle eyed Heath with a predatory study. "You must be Shelby's new squeeze."

"I am." He smiled. "Heath McLeroy." He offered

his hand to shake.

She returned the shake, holding his hand longer than necessary. I rolled my eyes and glanced at Cheryl.

"He's not on the menu, Michelle. Neither is Seth here. He's mine." She linked her arm through Seth's.

Michelle shrugged. "There are plenty of others for me to find. Take the man standing alone. He's cute enough. Not handsome, but still attractive. Those are the most easily influenced. Like Donald. Not homely enough to be desperate, but not good looking enough to be arrogant. These men are disposable. Watch and learn."

She swung her hips in the man's direction, faked a trip, and dropped her purse, all while falling into his arms. Of course, he caught her, then knelt to gather her spilled things. She tossed us a grin over her shoulder.

"She's despicable," Grandma said. "I bet she killed Donald."

"Shh." I motioned my head to the other women, but too late.

"You think Michelle killed him?" Jeanna's eyebrows rose. "Why?"

"Didn't you hear her? Men are disposable." Grandma stood and headed for the table loaded with casseroles.

Sasha watched her leave, then turned to me. "Are y'all trying to find the killer? I mean...I've heard of your success in the past, but never guessed you'd get involved in this one."

"I'm not." I stood. "Grandma is living a fantasy. Heath?"

"Wait." Sasha held up a hand. "You seriously aren't involved?"

"Well, I'd like to catch the person who did this, but I'm not actively looking. If I stumble across a clue, I'll turn it into the authorities." I dragged Heath to the food. "She's full of questions."

"Her fiancé was killed. Of course she's curious."

"Seems suspicious to me." I eyed all the different types of potatoes, choosing one with cheese and crushed potato chips on top. Then, I chose a fried chicken breast and a slice of cornbread. Nothing packs on the pounds like a Southern potluck.

By the time we returned to the table, Michelle was gloating. "I've got his phone number," she said. "He's very sweet."

"Try not to kill him," Jeanna muttered.

"Why would I do that?" Michelle's smile faded. "Are you insinuating I killed Donald?"

"Shelby's grandmother said it first."

"Oh, good grief. Just because I play with them then throw them away doesn't make me a killer."

Sasha cocked her head. "Weren't you upset when Donald left you?"

"Of course, but only because I do the leaving." She stared at April. "What's wrong with the little mouse at the end of the table?"

"It's a funeral!" April tossed down her napkin and

dashed from the building.

"Maybe she did it," Grandma said.

"Stop speculating." Mom glared. "You're causing problems."

Grandma crossed her arms. "There's nothing going on here. We might as well go home."

I agreed. I had a Christmas tree to decorate and children's tags to hang on the branches. "I'm ready whenever y'all are."

We clamored to our feet and made our way to the vehicles. I chose to ride with Heath, leaving Mom to drive Grandma, and Cheryl to ride with Seth. Even though I'd said I wouldn't investigate anymore, I wanted a chance to mull over the conversation at the table without Grandma's chatter.

Once Heath drove onto the highway, I said, "Who is your top suspect?"

"So, we are investigating?"

"No, just discussing."

"Michelle. She's a piranha. But then, quiet April might have. Still waters run deep, they say. Of course, Sasha has a temper simmering under that cool exterior. Then, Jeanna was wronged twice, right? So, yeah, I have no idea."

I laughed. "You're no help."

~

After changing into a pair of yoga pants and long tee shirt, I met the rest of my family and friends in the dining hall to set up the tree before supper. A stack of children's names and needs written on angel shaped tags, collected by Alice from a charitable organization, sat on a table. There were so many names, there wasn't much room for ornaments.

"Let's hang the tags with bows after stringing the lights. That's all we have room for. The children are the main cause anyway." I picked up the top tag. A five year old girl wanted a doll that looked real and a stroller. I tucked it into my pocket.

The next one was a three year old that wanted a Spiderman doll. I shoved that one in my pocket, too.

Heath chuckled. "If you keep doing that, there won't be any left for the rest of us."

"I wanted a boy and a girl. Now, I'm finished." I grinned and stepped back while he strung the lights. "With as many people living at Shady Acres now, I don't expect a single tag to be left on the tree."

"If there is, I'll cover them. No child deserves to not have something under the tree on Christmas morning."

"Helping children is the best idea Alice has ever had."

"It was your idea to do the tree," she said, coming up behind me. "Thank you. We'll have the wrapping party next weekend. We've plenty in the budget for paper and bows, but I'm going to ask the party store to donate as much as possible." She riffled through the names. "So many. It breaks my heart." She sighed.

"We'll give them a good Christmas, Alice." I put a hand on her shoulder. "There are wanted toys, clothes sizes, shoe sizes, everything we need to know."

"I'll make an announcement at supper for people to be generous. You'd better get a move on. Joyce doesn't like to serve the food late."

A quick glance at the clock showed we had an hour. Plenty of time. Once the lights were on, Mom, Grandma, Seth, Heath, Ted, and I had the tags hung in ten minutes. The tree looked pretty with angels hanging everywhere, white lights twinkling and red bows.

Heath slipped an arm around my waist. "It's beginning to look a lot like Christmas," he sang.

"Silly." I stood on tiptoe and kissed him. "Know what I want for Christmas?"

"I'm dying to know."

"A night out with you, away from everyone else. We're always surrounded by my family."

His hold tightened. "I agree. That sounds wonderful. Let's make it an entire weekend. I'll book a cabin in the mountains for the weekend after Christmas."

"Heaven."

"Not to spoil the romance," Seth said, "but I thought you might want to know we got DNA back from under Donald's nails."

I pulled free of Heath's embrace. "Whose?"

"They aren't in the system. We'll be taking DNA from all the jilted lovers. We're getting close." He grinned.

Hope that we'd find the killer by Christmas leaped

in my heart. Seth was going to catch the murderer, and I wasn't going to be in danger. What a wonderful holiday season!

As the residents filed into the dining hall, they made a beeline for the tree. Alice didn't have to make an announcement to guilt them into picking a name. All the names were gone before the last person sat down to eat.

Tears filled my eyes. I really did live amongst a wonderful group of people.

Bob Satchett, Mom's boyfriend, held a sprig of mistletoe over her head and kissed her. Her face turned a pretty shade of pink. I never would get used to such an unlikely pair getting together, but they were discreet. I needed to tell Mom it was okay by me. Dad had been gone a long time now. She deserved to be happy.

Ted grabbed the mistletoe and hung it over Grandma. She grabbed his face in her hands and planted a long kiss on his lips. I laughed when Seth then grabbed the plastic sprig and did the same with Cheryl.

"Our turn." Heath rushed forward.

The new kitchen help, Steve Olson, grabbed the mistletoe and sneaked a kiss from Alice. She gasped and slapped him. It didn't matter. He laughed as she stomped her way to her office.

Before I knew it, that little sprig had made its way around the room, filling the room with smiles and laughter. This was Christmas. This was joy. I wanted it all year long.

"Oh, I wish it was Christmas every day," Grandma said, echoing my thoughts. "Don't you, Teddy?"

"No, it's too expensive." He grinned, giving me a wink. He mouthed the word 'ring'.

He was buying Grandma a ring! I bounced in my seat, beyond thrilled.

My simple gift of copper insulated bottles that kept wine cool would be pale in comparison. I glanced at Heath. What could I buy for the best man on the planet?

Heath gave me that grin that melted my heart and I knew what he wanted. Three little words.

9

I pulled down a box from the top shelf of my closet and dug through the ugly Christmas sweaters given to me over the years. I chose one with a reindeer's head that had lights around his antlers. The lights ran off a small battery and blinked. The sweater was perfect for the gift-wrapping party.

Cheryl and I stepped out of our rooms at the same time, pointed at each other's sweaters, and laughed. Her's was a snowman whose stomach was stretched abnormally large over her chest.

"I know it's a little...tight, but it's the only ugly sweater I have." She tugged at the hem.

"It's ugly for sure. You're bound to win the contest."

'No, I won't. You're lit up like a deranged

Christmas tree."

We entered the dining hall where earlier Heath and I had set wrapping paper, tape, scissors and bows on every table. Christmas music played from a radio. Laughter and conversation flowed like fine champagne. The Jilted Ladies, I really needed to think of them as something different, congregated around the same table. The Christmas tree, bare of all its angels, sported only lights and red bows.

I rubbed my hands together, excited to participate, and joined my family at the table we usually sat at for meals. I gave Heath a kiss and a smile. "Merry Christmas. I'm going to tell you that every day. This room is filled with the spirit."

He pulled me into a one armed hug, his other busy holding a ribbon in place for Mom. "I'll take it."

"Nice sweater." His had dancing reindeer across a star-studded sky.

He laughed and released me. "Your gifts are under the table."

"Thanks." I pulled out the clothes and toys I'd bought for my two 'angels'.

Joyce and the kitchen staff brought out hot cider and hot chocolate, along with trays of Christmas cookies. Then, they joined the rest of us in wrapping gifts.

Grandma turned off the radio and started singing 'Silent Night'. Everyone joined in. I couldn't imagine a better Christmas party anywhere. Here, we were joined by a common goal—to provide a Christmas to a needy child. No one could stay unhappy in such circumstances.

"Did you think about the killer last night?" Grandma asked, shattering the illusion of peace.

I gave her a stern look and caught the gaze of Sasha who strolled by, a cup of cider in her hand. I smiled and waved. She glared and continued.

"Please don't ruin the party. I told you I left everything in Seth's hands. He's waiting on DNA results."

"Oh, pooh. I'll have to find something else for us to dig into after the holidays." She cut a long strip of silver ribbon. "I know you thought almost being eaten by a bear would curb the gumshoe bug that bit me, but it hasn't."

Mom sighed and kept her head bent over her wrapping. "We're doing the Lord's work here. No talk of death and murder."

"I'm pretty sure it was God that made me a thrill seeker, Sue Ellen." Grandma sniffed. "Who am I to deny his creation?"

Good grief. I tried not to laugh, I really did. But I couldn't help myself. My grandmother has some of the strangest ways of looking at things. "I'm going to get hot chocolate. Anyone want any?"

Everyone nodded. I slipped the scissors into the back pocket of my jeans so I'd have them when I returned, and headed for the dessert table.

"Shelby?"

I turned to face Sasha. "Merry Christmas."

She forced a smile. "Could you come help me with something, please? I bought a...rather large gift and can't bring it inside without help."

I eyed the pearl buttons on her snowy white sweater. "I'll get Heath." I turned to get him.

"No, no. You'll do." She grabbed my arm to stop me.

I shrugged. "Okay." I followed her outside, waiting for a chance to escape. "Where is it? I don't see anything?"

She heaved a sigh and pulled a small derringer from inside her sweater. "Let's walk the maze, shall we?"

I pulled out the button from my jeans. The same jeans I'd worn the day I found it. Opening my hand, I showed her. "You killed Donald?" My voice rose. Surely someone heard me?

"Not here. Proceed please." She prodded me in the back. "I wondered what happened to that button. They're antique, you know."

I glanced over my shoulder. No one seemed to know anything was amiss. With a groan, I headed through the cold night to the maze. I wrapped my arms around my middle and stopped at the entrance. "Where to?"

"The gazebo. Oh, yes, I know all about your favorite place to think. I've been watching you, Shelby Hart. From the moment I saw Donald reconnect. Now, move."

"You could have just let me go. I had no idea you were the one."

"Sure, you did. I saw the look you gave me back there."

The woman was nuts. "What look?"

"The one after the old lady started talking."

"That was a look of frustration!" I marched forward. Once we got to the gazebo, I needed to find a way of getting to the scissors in my pocket before she shot me. "Why the gun? You used lights on Donald."

"I'm not a killer. I lost control. The lights were handy. He put up quite a fight, once the initial shock wore off. Poor fool. He didn't know how good he could have had it, married to me." She giggled. "Too bad you're going to have to die wearing that sweater."

"Yeah, too bad." Except, I didn't plan on dying that night.

Once we got to the gazebo, I turned, pressing my back against the planked siding. "Was your fiancé really worth all this? He was nothing more than a cheat and a lier. If you put down the gun and walk away, I'll tell the others you went away for the holidays."

"Right. Then the cops will hound me for the rest of my life."

"Look, Sasha. They're going to hound you anyway. You killed one person, and now you plan on killing me. I have friends who are police officers. They won't stop until you're behind bars."

"Oh, sweetie." She gave a smile that chilled my blood. "I don't plan on going to jail. After I kill you, I'll shoot myself. There's no reason to go on without Donald. Not after what I've done. My life is ruined.

"When I saw him talking to you that day, I thought he wanted to get back with you. Rage filled me. I vowed he wouldn't make me a laughing stock as he did the rest of you. When he said he needed to talk to you again, I followed him. The garden was nice and dark that night, lit only by Christmas lights. It was actually kind of romantic."

"In a sick twisted way maybe. All he wanted from me was the gifts he'd given me during our engagement. He said he was getting married and needed them for his new fiancé."

"Really?" She put her free hand over her heart. "How sweet. But, it was a lie, too. He was so far in debt. I offered to help, but the man was too proud. Turn around, please."

"I don't think so. If you're going to shoot me, you can look in my eyes while you pull that trigger." I reached behind me for the scissors, wrapping my fingers around them.

She raised her gun hand.

I lunged forward, stabbing her in the forearm.

She screamed and dropped the gun.

As we scrambled for possession, sweet little Sasha spewed obscenities so vile, I swore my ears started bleeding. I kicked out at her, catching her in the thigh.

She was a little bigger than me, but I was a whole lot madder.

She grabbed my hair and yanked me back.

"Ow!" I swung at her jaw, connecting with a solid right fist.

She tackled me to the ground. "I'll just strangle you." Her fingers wrapped around my throat.

"Nope." I pulled my legs up between us and kicked off.

She went flying, landing on her back.

I jumped on top and straddled her, pinning her arms to her sides. "Now, you can be reasonable and stop trying to kill me, or I'll knock you out cold. Which is it?"

She spit in my face.

I grabbed a fist-sized rock and bashed her in the head. She went limp and I rolled off her, struggling to catch my breath.

I glanced at the night sky. "Okay, God. We haven't spoken in a good long while, but I'm getting kind of tired of this."

Taking a cue from Sasha's own handywork, I pulled a strand of lights from the gazebo and trussed her up like a Christmas hen. I brushed off my clothes and took a few steps toward the entrance.

"You're just going to leave me here?" Sasha whined. "It's cold."

"I don't care." The knuckles on my hand hurt, my head hurt, and she'd torn some lights off my sweater.

She could rot in the maze for all I cared. I picked up the gun and scissors and kept walking.

I'd just stepped from the maze when Heath and Seth raced toward me. Heath planted his hands on my shoulders, while Seth took the gun and scissors from my hands.

"What happened? Where's Sasha?" Heath asked.

"Tied up in the maze. She's certifiably nuts." I rested my forehead on his chest. "What took you two so long?"

"Seth showed up and said the DNA results matched Sasha's. I told him I'd seen you talking to her. We looked and couldn't find either one of you. We put two and two together. After searching the grounds, the only place left was the maze." He pulled me close. "Let's get you warm."

While Seth waved another police officer to follow him into the maze, Heath led me back to the dining hall. Ted shook his head when we entered and continued wrapping. Poor man. I used to be his headache before he retired from the force. Now, it looked as if I was Seth's problem.

Mom thrust a cup of hot chocolate into my hand while Heath lowered me to a chair. The rest of the Jilted Ladies crowded around.

"It was Sasha?" Michelle asked, eyes wide. "I never would have pegged her for a killer. I thought it was April."

"Me?" April frowned. "I wouldn't hurt a fly."

"That's why I thought it was you. It's the quiet people who are the craziest."

"At least no one thought it was me," Jeanna said.

"I did," I said. "For a moment. You still love him. I thought it might have been a crime of passion. But then, I suspected all of you."

Michelle laughed, attracting the attention of most of the residents. "No wonder you make the front page of our town paper so much. You're a riot!"

"Yeah, that's me." I sipped the chocolate, feeling warmth seep back into my bones.

"Back away. Let me through." Grandma squeezed through the women to my side. "You should have had me go with you. We could have tag teamed her."

"She asked for my help, then lured me like a lamb outside." Sometimes, I felt like the dullest crayon in the box.

We all turned as Seth and the officer dragged a handcuffed Sasha into the room. Seth sat her forcibly into a chair and left the other man to guard her. "You all right?" He asked.

"I'm fine. She ruined my sweater." I stuck my finger in a hole where a light had once been.

"It was ugly anyway." Seth grinned. "From the looks of the two of you, it must have been quite the fight."

"We rolled around on the ground like a couple of animals." I glanced with satisfaction to where the side of Sasha's head was matted with blood. "She's tougher than she looks."

"So are you apparently." He clapped a hand on my shoulder. "Do you need an ambulance?"

"No, just a hot shower."

"A glass of wine wouldn't hurt," Grandma said. "It'll loosen you up."

"No thank you." I held out my hand to Heath. "Let's leave this place. The others can clean up. I've had enough festivities for one night. Seth, I'll be in tomorrow to fill out my forms."

With Heath's arm around me, we shuffled back to my cottage. It didn't take long for all my bumps and bruises to make themselves known. Heath drew me a bubble bath, poured me a glass of diet soda, and kissed me. "Thank you for making life interesting."

I smiled. "My pleasure."

Epilogue

*C*hristmas morning dawned crisp and bright. My suitcase, packed and ready for the weekend rested in the corner of my bedroom. Through the bedroom door, the twinkling lights on my tabletop tree cast flickering colors along the hardwood floor. I tossed off my blankets and shuffled to the front room.

Heath, Cheryl, Mom, and Grandma were already gathered around the tree, cups of coffee in their hands. Heath handed me one, along with a kiss. "Merry Christmas, sleepyhead."

"Merry Christmas," I murmured. "Presents?"

Under the tree were several gaily wrapped gifts. Some I'd put there, others I hadn't.

"Let's toast to the birthday of our Lord," Mom said, raising her mug. "And thank him that my crazy daughter is here to enjoy another holiday."

"Here here!" I clinked my cup against hers. "Who wants to play Santa?"

"I will." Heath started handing out gifts. When he'd finished, he took his and sat on the sofa next to me. "Ida, you go first."

"Oldest first, huh?" She grinned and ripped into the gift from me. "I've wanted the wine cooler bottles for ages. Thank you, Shelby."

"I know I shouldn't encourage you, but I couldn't resist." I smiled.

Mom got her several pairs of outlandish colored leggings, Cheryl gave her a journal, and Heath presented her with a faux fur stole. Grandma couldn't be happier. "Thank you all for the gifts, but I have to be honest and say Teddy's to me last night is the best by far." She wiggled the 2-carat diamond ring on her finger.

"I love the earrings Bob gave me." Mom flicked the ruby in her ear. "You need to get to know him better, Shelby. He's very sweet."

"We're poker partners, Mom. I know him very well, and yes, he is."

After the others had opened their gifts, I presented Heath with a small box. He raised his eyebrows and opened it. Inside, rested a single sheet of paper on which I'd written the words, 'I love you'. If he knew me as well as I thought he did, he'd know how much those words actually cost me.

He grinned, his eyes shimmering. "I was going to wait until this weekend, but…" He pulled a box from his pocket and stood, pulling me to my feet. "Shelby Hart, I know you've been wounded. I know commitment is hard for you. I know what it cost you to say those words, well, sort of say them," he gave a crooked smile. "So, I'm not asking for this to happen right now. I'll wait forever if I have to, but will you wear this ring and proclaim to the world that you're my girl? The woman who will someday, Lord willing, be my wife?" He lifted the lid.

Inside sparkled a simple solitary diamond of a princess cut. He knew me so well. I lifted eyes filled with tears. "Yes, someday, I will marry you. I can't promise when."

He chuckled. "Just try and live long enough, okay?"

I giggled. "That I can promise to try and do." I caressed his face. Early morning stubble rasped against my palm. "Thank you for waiting, for being so patient. You've made this the best Christmas ever."

He lowered his head and kissed me to whoops and hollers from the other three. I tuned them out and wrapped my arms around his neck. Thank you, God, for the gift of Heath.

The End

Scan the code for the next book, Deadly Greenhouse Gases

ABOUT THE AUTHOR

Website at www.cynthiahickey.com
Also www.forgetmenotromances.com

Multi-published and Amazon Best-Selling author Cynthia Hickey had three cozy mysteries and two novellas published through Barbour Publishing. Her first mystery, Fudge-Laced Felonies, won first place in the inspirational category of the Great Expectations contest in 2007. Her third cozy, Chocolate-Covered Crime, received a four-star review from Romantic Times. All three cozies have been re-released as ebooks through the MacGregor Literary Agency, along with a new cozy series, all of which stay in the top 50 of Amazon's ebooks for their genre. She had several historical romances release through Harlequin's Heartsong Presents, and has sold close to a million copies of her works since 2013. She has taught a Continuing Education class at the 2015 American Christian Fiction Writers conference. You can find her on FB, twitter, and Goodreads, and is a contributor to Cozy Mystery Magazine blog and Suspense Sisters blog. She and her husband run the small press, Forget Me Not Romances, which includes some of the CBA's best well-known authors. She lives in Arizona with her husband, one of their seven children, two dogs, two cats, three box turtles, and two Sulcata tortoises. She has seven grandchildren who keep her busy and tell everyone they know that "Nana is a writer".